Copyright © 2000 by Berenstain Enterprises, Inc.
All rights reserved under International and Pan-American Copyright Conventions.
Published in the United States by Random House, Inc., New York, and simultaneously
in Canada by Random House of Canada Limited, Toronto.

www.randomhouse.com/kids   www.berenstainbears.com

Library of Congress Cataloging-in-Publication Data
Berenstain, Stan, 1923–
The Berenstain Bears: That stump must go! / by Stan & Jan Berenstain.
   p. cm. "Beginner books."
SUMMARY: Papa Bear is determined to remove a hazardous tree stump from the front
yard no matter what it takes.
ISBN 0-679-88963-9 (trade). — ISBN 0-679-98963-3 (lib. bdg.)
[1. Bears—Fiction. 2. Trees—Fiction.   3. Roots (Botany)—Fiction.
4. Father—Fiction. 5. Stories in rhyme.]
I. Berenstain, Jan, 1923– . II. Title.
PZ8.3.B4493Bhjd   2000   [E]—dc21   97-40641
Printed in the United States of America   August 2000   10 9 8 7 6 5 4 3 2 1

BEGINNER BOOKS, RANDOM HOUSE, and colophons are registered trademarks
of Random House, Inc.

The Berenstain Bears
THAT STUMP MUST GO!

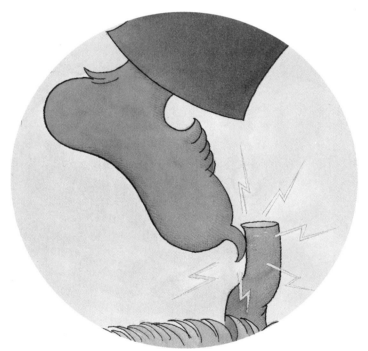

Stan & Jan Berenstain

BEGINNER BOOKS®
A Division of Random House, Inc.

OUCH!

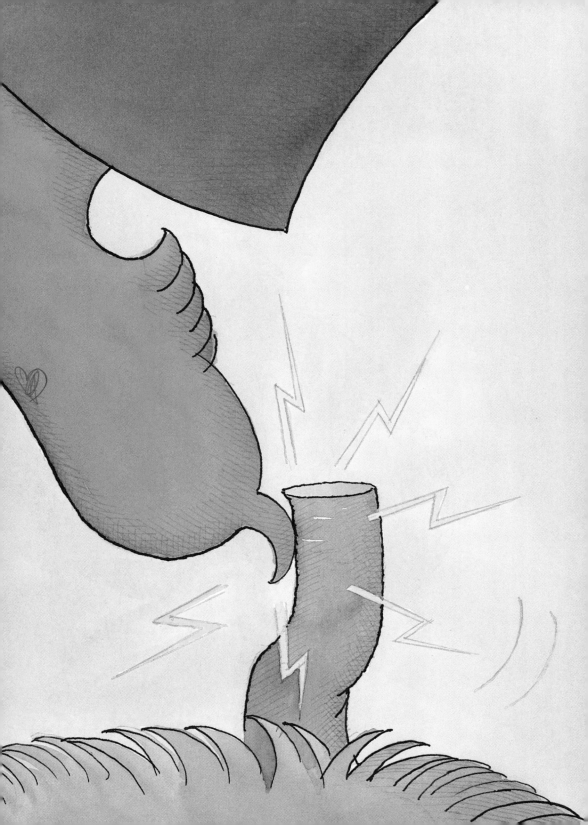

That small stump
hurt my toe!
That small stump
has got to go!

Help! Help!
The ground just shook!
What happened?
I'm afraid to look!

Papa Bear
has hurt his toe.
Papa says
that stump must go.

That stump is small,
Papa Bear.
Why not just
leave it there?

It must go,
small or big.
To remove it,
I will have to dig.

And dig and dig
and dig and dig!

You are a good
digger, Pop.
But that stump is just
small on top.
Underneath,
it's pretty big.

That does not matter.
Not at all.
I'll get it out,
roots and all!

Don't worry, friends.
You just heard Papa Bear.
He'll get it all
out of there.

When he starts,
he does not stop.
That's one good thing
about my pop.

My pop is strong.

He pulls hard.

He'll pull those roots

out of your yard!

See? See?
He pulled so hard
the roots are gone
from your yard!

Wow! A tougher stump
you'll never face.
Can you remove it
from its place?

I can. I must
go after it!
No stump, no roots
can make me quit!

To remove a stump,
you dig and chop!
To get it out,
you must not stop!

Papa says

he will not stop.

No stump, no roots

can stop my pop.

Psst! Psst!

Papa Bear!

Roots and all,

that stump's still there!

But not for long!
Not much longer!
It may be strong,
but dynamite
is much, much stronger!

Papa Bear, that was
some ker-whump,
but it did not seem
to hurt the stump.

That stump is strong,
I do not doubt.
But this machine
will get it out.

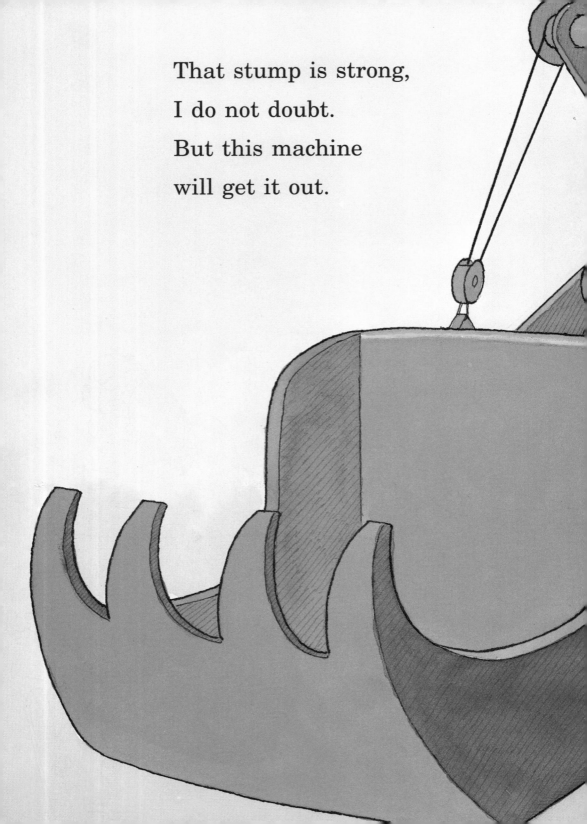

I said it before,
because it is so.
That stump,
those roots,
that mess
must...

Pop did it, Ma!

Isn't that good?

He removed that stump

from the neighborhood!